FIRST FIXER

A GARY BLOODFIST NOVELLA

JAMES JAKINS

My NAME IS Garack Bloodfist and I am an orc. Full-blooded, strong, proud. You can call me Gary.

The story I'm going to tell you took place about a year after my family had relocated to the city of Summervale, Virginia. How did orcs end up in Virginia? Well, that's a potentially longer story that involves lying wizards, angry gods, and a small bit of inter-dimensional travel. The important takeaway from that story, though, is that you need to know a guy.

I know a guy. In fact, I know a few. The wizard that opened the doorway for us was just one; I'm also poker-buddies with the best damn butcher this side of the Mississippi, and happen to be on a first-name basis with a drow princess pretending to be a detective—I'll get to her—but for the sake of this story, because we have to start somewhere, I want to tell you about the guys from poker night.

I learned a long time ago that when it comes to cards, it's sometimes a good idea to lose. Especially when the others around the table are wealthy and/or connected.

I know that might sound counterintuitive, but trust me, you get a lot more from people if they're happy to see you. They tend to be less happy to see you if every time they do you take their money.

I know, I know, that shouldn't be an issue at a friendly game among friends, but I'd learned to play cards with other orcs. I'd gotten tired of having to beat the shit out of friends every time I won a hand, so I made sure I lost more than I won and I kept my new friends happy to see me.

One of the first things I learned when we arrived on Earth was that all the most important decisions were made by fat old men sitting around a table smoking cigars and drinking cheap alcohol—not too different from the last world, really. And while the decisions made in this room were not world-changing, they occasionally changed the world for individuals.

I folded—a pair of kings—and Larry laughed as he slid the pile of bills from the middle of the table to his own slowly growing pile.

"King high, boys." He dropped his worthless hand on the table and we all groaned dramatically.

The cards were gathered up and Ed—the butcher I told you about—shuffled the deck. "So what's happening with your latest crew, Larry?" Ed asked as he began to deal the cards.

"Fuck 'em," Larry said as he inspected his new hand.

"What's that?" I asked. Larry owned a local construction company, and lately business had been doing pretty well for him. So well that he'd recently had to outsource the labor for a few of his sites.

Larry shook his head. "Got a call this morning. New

2

crew didn't show up at the site so the foreman went round to the motel. Figured it had just been a rough first night at the Bearded Lady. Nothing. Bastards had just packed up and left town."

Sam—Summervale's fifth-best barber, out of five— let out a humorless laugh. "Well, that's what you get for hiring a crew from West Virginia. No work ethic up there. If it's not coal or welfare they don't give a shit."

Our final player, Ben, shook his head. "Probably just got offered higher pay somewhere else." Ben stood out from the rest of the players in the dimly lit, smoke-filled room. For one, he was better-dressed, in a well-tailored suit and custom-made shoes. Helped that his family owned half the city. The other way he was different was that he was a gnome.

No one seemed to care about that. If anyone suspected the man was anything other than a very short human, they didn't say anything about it. What they did care about was the fact that the son of a bitch was loaded.

They all mumbled their agreement to Ben's observation. I sat and considered Larry's situation.

"What exactly did you need the crew for?" I asked after everyone else had settled down.

Larry gave me a look that a year before might have ended with him bleeding out on the floor. "To build shit, Gary."

I rolled my eyes. "What shit, Larry?"

Larry seemed to be considering another snarky comment, but thought better of it. "Thought I'd mentioned it before, but there's a little housing project

3

on the edge of town. Cookie-cutter houses the whole way. I won the bid for a few lots."

"And I'm guessing you just need bodies?" I asked.

Larry shrugged. "At this point anyone that can swing a hammer or hold a wall up would be good enough."

Ben spared me a quick glance over his cards. "You know, Larry," he said, rearranging his hand, "I happen to know that our good friend Gary has some rather large cousins."

"It's true," I agreed, offering Ben a grateful smile. My brother worked for Ben on his ranch. Kaga had been the fist's Warg-tamer. By comparison, horses were the easiest thing in the world to break. Ben was aware of what I was. Even if I was the first orc he'd ever met, he knew what it meant.

Kaga's position on Ben's ranch had been my first successful job placement attempt. It was partially my fault we were stuck here, so I saw it as my responsibility to make sure everyone lived as comfortably as possible.

Larry seemed to grasp the unspoken message in Ben's statement. He gave me serious consideration. "They as big as you are?"

I grinned. "Some are even bigger."

TWO

THE NEXT MORNING, per Larry's instructions, I took a couple of my fellow orcs to the new development.

Hurck and Rit Slayinghand had not been very happy with my assault on their apartment door so early in the morning, but when I told them I'd found them work they shut up pretty quickly.

Neither of the Slayinghand siblings had managed to hold down a job for very long. Most recently both of them had been fired, on the same day, from both of Summervale's McDonalds. Hurck for eating on the job —frowned upon, apparently—and Rit for shouting back when a customer complained.

I explained the job to them as we drove. They both seemed relieved to hear that it mostly required picking things up and moving them. Hurck was also experienced with construction, having once served in a mercenary company as one of their siege engine technicians—that's not actually what they called them, but it sounds more impressive on a resume. Her brother didn't have that experience, but I had faith in both of them.

I parked my car—an Escort held together by wire and duct tape—next to Larry's brand new pickup.

He must have heard us coming because he met us by the cars just as we were climbing out.

"Gary! Glad you could make it. These your cousins?" He managed to make the question sound legitimate. Anyone would be able to tell that. We aren't actually related, but there is still a familial resemblance in every orc. At least, there is if you're human and don't know what features to look for.

"That's right. Hurck, Rit, this is Larry. He's agreed to give you a trial run on his current project. I've talked you up, so don't fuck this job up too, alright?"

The two orcs gave me warning glares that told me it was too early in the morning to try to throw my weight around. They were at least well-mannered enough to offer Larry a few words of forced gratitude for the opportunity.

"Of course, of course." Larry turned from us and shouted across the bare dirt toward the slab of concrete waiting for walls to go up. "Jerem! Get over here."

A young man in a baseball cap, jeans, and nothing else rushed over. "What's up, Larry?"

Beside me Hurck made a pleased sound at the sight of the well-muscled young human. I don't think anyone else noticed...

Larry introduced Jerem to Rit and Hurck and instructed him to get them started on the site. The young man nodded his understanding and led the two off.

It didn't take long before Hurck had pushed her brother out of the way and was leaning down to whisper something in the man's ear. I held my breath as I watched, and let it out, relieved, when the response was a loud, natural laugh.

"You didn't tell me one of your cousins was going to be a woman," Larry said reproachfully.

"I didn't think it would matter. I mean, look at her." I indicated Hurck as she incited another head-thrown-back laugh from the young human. She was more muscled than any of the topless sunburned men currently on site.

I occasionally forgot about the strange stigma a lot of humans had concerning gender, but even if I had thought of it, I still would have chosen her and Rit for this job. I had to put the best recruits forward. Once they established their worth, Larry would likely ask for others. Then I would leave it up to the Slayinghand siblings to select others from within the fist that they thought would be able to fill the positions.

Larry shook his head. He obviously didn't care. "Fine. They have today, maybe tomorrow to prove they're worth anything. Either way, I appreciate your bringing them over for me." Larry extended a hand and I accepted it. Larry was big, for a human, and his grip was strong.

"Anytime, Larry. I appreciate the offer. If I'm being honest, they've had some bad luck holding down employment. But I think this is a good fit. Wish we'd considered it sooner."

Business concluded, I pulled out a pack of cigarettes and offered one to Larry, which he accepted. We stood in silence and smoke for a while and watched the crew.

Hurck now had an entire flock of young, shirtless

men laughing at what I'm assuming was a very inappropriate story.

Our smoke break was interrupted by the sound of a car pulling off the road into the lot.

Larry and I turned to see a dull brown sedan. From the driver-side door a man in his early thirties climbed out. I hate to say this about the man, but he was the dullest-looking person I had ever seen. I got to know him in later years, and I have to say, Detective Matt Fitzpatrick is one of the best men I know, but when you look at him standing next to his partner, he just seems so insignificant.

The passenger door opened and a dark-skinned woman stepped out. Her eyes darted around the lot and seemed to devour every piece of information that was available.

Whatever gods had populated my birth-world must have been responsible for this one as well, because I recognized her for an elf immediately—the sharp face with its upturned nose and high cheekbones. And the brown of her eyes wasn't right. I can't really explain it. But it was a color that *almost* looked like it belonged. This was the first time I'd ever met Denelle Halldorson. A year in Summervale, and I was only just now learning the city had at least one elf. It made me happy that Jackson had brought us here, for some reason.

In the old world, elves and orcs didn't really get along, but we respected each other. For me, the presence of elves meant that there was magic in the world. More than wizards and dragons, elves have always represented that to me. I can't even really put into words why.

The problem with this belief of mine, though, was

that it made that first meeting not as pleasant as it could have been.

The two of them, after exiting the car, approached us. I apparently had an excited smile on my face at the sight of the elf and she glared at me as they approached.

"What are you looking at?" she demanded.

The human glanced at her, then to me. He spoke before I could answer. "Sorry about that, she's new. Are either of you Larry Cochran?"

"That'd be me. What can I do for you?"

The man tapped at a small golden shield on his belt. "I'm Detective Fitzpatrick, this is my partner, Detective Halldorson. We were hoping we could ask you a few questions."

"About what?" Larry asked, confused.

"A missing van full of construction workers," Halldorson answered for him. She was still glaring at me.

"What?" Larry said.

Both detectives were looking at me now. "Maybe you'd like to have this conversation in private?" Fitzpatrick asked.

Larry looked at me and I shrugged. He shook his head. "No, he's a friend, it's fine."

"Okay." Fitzpatrick looked to Halldorson and nodded for her to continue.

"You had a crew that was supposed to show up at this site yesterday, correct?"

"Yeah." Larry nodded. "Bastards didn't even call to let us know they weren't going to make it. Just packed up and left town. Why you asking?"

"We got a report from the manager of the motel they

were staying at that they never paid for their stay. Then a maid found blood in one of the rooms."

Larry and I let out streams of smoke as we said, as one, "Oh."

"We reached out to their local police department and they were able to confirm that they never made it back home. We were hoping you could shed some light on the situation for us."

"God damn," Larry said softly as he rolled his cigarette between his thumb and middle finger. Finally he shook his head. "I never even met them. Just got a call from their guy in West Virginia that they were on their way. He gave me their room info so I could have one of our guys show them around town. You know what?" He snapped his fingers as he remembered something. "Let me grab Trevor for you. He was supposed to show them around a few nights ago. You okay waiting here?"

They nodded and he hurried off to find Trevor.

After he was out of earshot Detective Halldorson turned her full attention back to me. "What are you?" she asked.

"Den!" Fitzpatrick said, obviously embarrassed by his partner's lack of tact.

She ignored him. "You're definitely not human, but I don't think I've ever seen… whatever you are, before."

I grinned. I was used to this sort of question. Anytime I met another non-human in Summervale, they asked. Orcs didn't exist in this world. Not before we showed up, anyway.

"Well, I wouldn't want to offend an elf, now would I?" I asked.

Her eyes narrowed. "Just answer my question."

"Well, if you must know, I'm an orc."

She stared at me suspiciously. "Orcs aren't real."

"And yet, here I am."

Any further questioning was cut off as Larry returned with another young man in tow. "Trevor, this is Detective... uh..." He looked to the detectives to introduce themselves again. "They have a few questions about the West Virginia crew you took out a few nights ago."

"Oh, shit, did something happen to them?" Trevor asked. "Is that why they're not here?"

"That's what we want to find out." Fitzpatrick dug around in a pocket of his cheap suit jacket and pulled out a folded photo. He unfolded it and showed it to Trevor. "That's them, right?"

I glanced over Trevor's shoulder and studied the faces of the five young men. One wore a hat with a confederate flag on it, another had a burn mark on one cheek. Nothing to really distinguish them beyond that, but I've never been good at telling humans apart.

"That's them," Trevor said.

"Great. Mind if we ask you some questions?"

"Go for it."

"If that'll be all..." Larry started to step away from the detectives.

"Oh, of course. Thank you, Mr. Cochran. If you think of anything else," Fitzpatrick handed Larry a card. "Just give that number a call, alright?"

"Of course. And you let me know if I can help in any way."

I chose that time to make my exit as well. I gave my

friendliest head nod to the detectives, and offered one final grin to the elf, and climbed inside my car.

Through the glass of the window I could hear Larry shouting at his crew to get back to work.

THREE

AT THIS POINT in the story you might be asking some questions. I don't know if I'll have satisfactory answers for some of them, but there is one I can answer: How did a bunch of orcs from another world learn English?

That's easy. We didn't. Well, I didn't. Some of the others did. But those of us without the patience for it cheated. We had a wizard cast a spell on us.

Josh Maine doesn't like being called a wizard. He prefers the term Magician. "Wizards spend too much time punching things," he likes to say.

I should point out that he didn't cast the spell for free, either. The payment he asked for might sound a little strange, but it was that we attended the weekly ESL course that he taught at the local community college.

That might seem counter-intuitive, but Professor Maine warned us that the spell he'd cast would wear off eventually, and if we really wanted to be able to speak English, we should take his class. If we went to the class every Thursday night, he reasoned, by the time the spell wore off we'd actually know what we were talking about.

On this particular Thursday night we all sat waiting for Professor Maine to finish the arcane symbol he was outlining on the classroom's blackboard. We talked and gossiped as the chalk scraped.

Half the classroom was full of orcs, all of us doing our best to not break the woefully inadequate desks. A lot of us had gained weight after a year of prepackaged potato chips and fast food, which made squeezing in between the chair and the desk a bit of a challenge.

The other half was full of our goblin comrades. Even after all this time, they still enjoyed watching us struggle with the tight fit.

I did my best to ignore the snickering assholes and spoke, instead, with Hurck.

"Went well, then?" I asked her.

"I'd say so. Rit and I framed a whole room while Larry had his back turned. He offered us full-time jobs."

I smiled at that. "I knew you'd impress him. Just don't go and break any of his boys, alright?"

"No promises." Her grin was wicked and full of unspoken promises I knew she'd keep.

I remembered the other excitement from the site and asked after the detectives. "Did you happen to see the elf that stopped by?"

"The dark one?" she asked.

"Yeah."

She nodded. "Yeah. Trevor told us they were asking about some other crew that was supposed to be helping with the job, but they vanished. Something about blood in their room. He didn't give too many details. Sounds like something happened to them, though." She didn't seem too concerned about the disappearance of five men.

I wasn't really, either. We'd grown up wading through blood, and death didn't really have the same meaning to us that it probably did to humans. But having spent a good portion of my life being blamed for every horrible thing that happened—to be fair, I *was* responsible for some of it—I liked to stay apprised of these things.

That elf had given me a look that very loudly proclaimed, "I don't trust you." So I wanted to make sure to get ahead of any situation that might bring trouble our way.

"Do me a favor and let me know if she or her partner stop by to ask any more questions, alright?"

Hurck cocked her head as she considered the request. "Sure," she said finally. "Know something we don't?"

I shook my head. "Not yet. Just don't trust lawmen."

This answer made her grin again. "That's cause you're not as stupid as you look."

FOUR

THAT THURSDAY NIGHT was an eventful one. After class let out I made my way to the Bearded Lady. The Bearded Lady is Summervale's best bar. I say best because it's the most welcoming to hulking orcs who drink too much and start fights.

The fights are usually with the other orcs in the room, so the other patrons tend to be more understanding than they could have been. And, I'm proud to say, the fights are getting less frequent.

My brother, Kaga, met me inside. He waved me over with two amber bottles and placed one in front of me as I sat down on the stool next to him.

"How was class?" he asked in Orcish.

"You'd know if you joined us once in a while," I responded in English.

He shrugged. "Learning enough fancy talk on the ranch."

Kaga was surrounded by other immigrants. Others that, like us, were trying to start a new life. He always said they seemed to do just fine without English. I didn't think that was entirely true, but I let him lie to himself. It's what a good brother does.

Hanging on the wall behind the bar a TV was silently sharing that evening's late night news.

I spared it enough of a glance to see the face of a young woman and the word "Missing" prominently displayed.

"I think there's something going on in this town, Kaga," I said to my brother in Orcish.

He took note of my Orcish and followed my gaze to the screen. "Because a girl went missing? Shit like that happens, brother."

I shook my head. "It shouldn't. But that's not what I mean." I told him about the missing crew.

"An elf lawman?" he asked.

"That was my initial takeaway, too. Again, though, not the point I'm trying to make."

He sighed as he took a drink. "Look, Garack, I'm saying this as your brother. Your older, much more handsome brother. Don't get involved. You know how it goes. We make damn good suspects anytime someone needs to be blamed. And I know you thought that already, and that's why you want to do something. But doing anything will just put you out there for that elf to see and decide you look the part of a kidnapping murderer." He took another drink. "Besides, this is just a couple humans disappearing. No one has any proof of foul play. Am I right?"

I shrugged. There had been blood found in one of the rooms, but maybe Kaga was right.

We settled back into silence, enjoying our drinks and the quiet conversations of our fellow patrons.

The bar was never packed, but it usually had a decent crowd—the usual collection of sad sacks drinking alone and men and women of various races trying to fill their empty places with another's company.

A few stools down from us a few men of the latter variety were attempting to convince a woman that she would enjoy their company. She didn't seem to believe them.

"I'm not interested. Thank you." She didn't look at them as she answered, but turned in her stool to try to make the rejection more obvious.

"You know, I get the feeling that you think we're asking." One of the men dropped a large, calloused hand on her shoulder.

She rose quickly and attempted to walk away. Another of the three men grabbed her wrist and pulled her back.

The woman let out a short cry and punched the man in the face. His head turned slightly from the blow, but that was about it.

He stared down at her, a malicious grin spreading across his face and he leaned down toward her, mouth opening.

That was when Kaga and I stepped in. My brother's hand fell on the man's arm and he not-so-gently turned him away from the woman.

The man looked down at my brother—Kaga is incredibly short for an orc, standing a little under six feet. "Mind your own business, man."

Kaga smiled up at the man and answered in broken English. "Lady not interested. Maybe you and friends should go home."

19

I did my job as the more intimidating specimen and stepped up behind Kaga with my arms folded across my chest.

Instead of scaring them away like it normally would, the three of them just started laughing. The jackass in the confederate flag hat did release the girl's arm and let her get away as he turned his full body toward us. The other two took up positions behind us.

"This should be fun," one of them said. I glanced over my shoulder and noted a burn mark on his cheek.

"Much fun," Kaga said, right before he threw the first punch.

There's no honor in waiting for your opponent to swing first. That's how you lose a fight. If you know there's going to be violence, the best course of action is to make sure you're the one doing that violence before the other guy realizes it's coming.

My brother might not be big, as orcs go, but he is strong. And he's not one to pull a punch. That's another sure way to lose a fight. So when the man merely stumbled back a step or two instead of collapsing in a pile of limp limbs and broken teeth, the two of us were understandably surprised.

In fact, most of the bar went silent. Orcs had been supporting the Bearded Lady for a year now, and the regulars knew what we could do. Now we all stared, mouths open, as the man straightened up, wiped the non-existent blood from his mouth, and laughed.

Now, I should point out that it's not impossible for humans to be that strong. I've seen it before. Our home world was home to an order of powerful paladins. Even without their god's blessing they were powerful warriors, and I've met wizards and barbarians that could hit harder than some orcs. But that was my world. Even there I'd never seen a human stand up after being hit by my brother, let alone one that didn't go down.

It was while the three of them were laughing and the rest of the bar was staring in shocked silence that my instincts started screaming at me to get moving.

Another important rule about fighting, maybe the most important, is that you should never expect a fair fight. And you should never expect a fair fight because you should do everything within your power to make sure the fight is as one-sided as possible. Weapons are always preferable, and, when necessary, improvised weaponry is a damn fine option.

I moved a fraction of an instant before the men behind me did. As I spun to face them I shot my hand out and pulled a bottle off the bar. The contents sloshed inside as I swung it directly into the temple of the first man in its path.

There was an explosion of brown glass and a mist of unfinished beer around the man's face.

His eyes opened wide as the force of my swing managed to lift him from his feet and throw him to the ground.

His buddy didn't even wait for him to hit the ground before he threw his own punch at my face.

His fist moved faster than any human has a right to move, and I only just managed to throw my arms up in a defensive stance. Did me no good, though. One second I was standing, the next I was flat on my back, head ringing like a broken bell.

I was vaguely aware of Kaga shouting in surprise, and then the sound of wood splintering.

My vision cleared in time to see the man with the confederate flag hat bending over me. I shook my head again, because for a moment I thought his eyes were red. When I looked again it was confirmed. Red eyes.

"Oh fuck." I must have said it out loud because the man's grin widened. And there they were. His teeth, two of them. Longer and sharper than was strictly necessary.

Old muscle memory kicked in and I swung my hand up. I was still holding the neck of the broken bottle, so I shoved it as deeply as I could into the red eye.

The man jumped back, screaming in pain, and he turned away from me, hands flying up to remove the shard of glass.

I kicked out as hard as I could with both feet and hit him in the back of the knee.

The strike must have surprised him because he fell backwards, legs collapsing underneath him.

I rolled out of the way and jumped to my feet. I threw my hands up, ready to keep going, even though I knew it was pointless. I'd fought vampires before. If you didn't come prepared, well... if you didn't come prepared you were basically fucked.

"That's enough!" We all spun to find Danyl Ironbeard, the owner and manager of the bar, waving a shotgun in the air. Behind him was his wife, Kide, and the girl the men had been bothering earlier. The girl's eyes were wide with fear, and I had a feeling she was going to collapse the second her adrenaline let up.

The three men laughed again. The sight was made worse by the now rising figure with the bloody glass shard sticking out of his face. They took a step toward the owner and the two women.

Danyl Ironbeard was a dwarf, even if he was clean-shaven, and just like in my world, the dwarves of Earth never backed down from a fight. He also stepped forward, and leveled the gun at the lead figure.

"Don't," I said as I stepped between the dwarf and the vampire. Not in front of the gun—I let the barrel go under my arm and keep its line on the figure, but I wanted to be ready if the shot did nothing and the thing jumped.

All three of them stepped closer, and their eyes must have been visible to the dwarf now, because I could hear his intake of breath.

"Oh, shite." He shoved the gun up toward me. "Hold this."

I grabbed the barrel without thinking and pulled it up and aimed it right at the flag on the lead man's hat.

Behind me Danyl spun around and there was a gasp from Kide. "Sorry, love, gonna need this."

He stepped around me and advanced on the three men. I glanced down and saw a silver chain dangling from his hand. In his grasp was a small silver cross.

The three vampires froze. Their faces twisted in disgust. Under the surface of their skin I could see the distortion, like something crawling around, trying to break through.

They must be young vampires, I thought. The stronger ones would transform when exposed to a holy symbol.

"Get out of my bar. You are not welcome here." Ironbeard stepped closer and the three screamed.

They covered their eyes with their arms and turned and rushed out the door. The first to reach it didn't even bother opening it, just hit it at full speed and pulled the heavy thing off its hinges, flinging it into the street.

Against the far wall I could hear groaning. I turned to see Kaga, with the help of a few patrons, freeing himself from the wreckage of a table.

"What in all the hells was that, brother?" he asked in Orcish.

"Bloodsuckers." I didn't say vampire because it's the same in English and Orcish, and I didn't want to cause a scene. I knew perfectly well how people reacted when they heard that word.

Kaga didn't respond, just dropped to the floor again and ran a hand through his hair.

I handed Danyl his gun back. "I think you should put a few more of those up." I indicated the cross.

He nodded. "They won't be back. Just babies by the look of them."

"You have some experience with them?"

He shrugged. "So do you, from the looks of it."

"I have experience with a lot of things. Some I never expected to see here."

"Well, thanks for your help." He turned from me, and in a louder voice addressed the bar. "Alright, everybody. I think we're going to be closing early tonight."

Everyone looked from him to the broken door. No one seemed very eager to leave. I couldn't blame them.

FIVE

KAGA and I spent the remainder of our night escorting young women to their cars and answering questions asked by the two cops that had showed up responding to a call made by one of the patrons.

They'd immediately assumed Kaga and I had been responsible for the damages, but Danyl had been able to convince them that we were actually the heroes of the evening.

It was well after midnight when I finally made it home.

Our apartment at the time was small. There was a single bedroom—reserved for me and the wife—a living room barely big enough for the couch, and the kitchen with its small table.

The bedroom door was closed—Pat was likely already asleep—so I sat on the couch next to my sister, who also lived with us.

"What happened to you?" Shakill asked, waving a finger over her own face in approximately the same location the vampire had punched me.

I considered telling her, but sleeping on the floor, in little nests they'd made out of pillows and blankets, were my son Garack and my nephew Lukill. The two were snoring gently, faces illuminated by the flickering light from the TV. Since arriving in this world, the two of them rarely, if ever, moved away from the screen. They were constantly watching shows filled with bright colors and screaming men with hair that changed color. They adored it. They didn't even complain when my sister stole the remote and chose another show, though she was fine watching anything as well.

Instead of answering her question I shook my head. "I'll tell you later." I indicated the boys and she nodded in understanding. Some conversations aren't meant for young ears.

We sat without talking for a while and just watched the flashing images on our small TV.

I hadn't realized quite how late it was until the early morning news fired up.

"Shit, is it really four?" I asked Shakill.

She shrugged and took a swig from a beer can in response.

I sighed and settled back into the couch. The news was basically just a repeat of the reports that had been playing on the bar's TV as well, but I watched and read the headlines.

I sat up straight when the talking head mentioned a group of men from West Virginia that had apparently gone missing several days earlier. The reporter questioned whether or not there was a connection between the five men and the missing girl.

The part that caught my eye was the image they

displayed on the top corner. It was a picture I'd seen early Thursday morning at Larry's construction site. A picture of five men. One of the men was wearing a hat with a confederate flag. Another had a burn mark on one cheek.

This was probably some sort of sign that I needed to do something about the situation.

SIX

I FEEL like I need to backtrack a little at this point. Anyone that knows my history is likely aware of what I did for a living before we moved to Summervale.

For those that don't: I was a bandit. A damn good one, too. I led the orc fist, as well as our goblin allies, in countless successful raids. The price on my head was enough that anyone who did manage to kill me would have lived comfortably for a while.

What a lot of people don't know is that I didn't start out as a bandit. I don't think most people do.

My first job was a common one for orcs. I joined a group of mercenaries. Sometimes we were called adventurers. Basically, we went from town to town and took coin in exchange for killing someone or something.

It wasn't a large group. There were only five of us, but we were good at what we did. And our specialty was killing monsters.

And yes, that includes vampires.

You never forget your first vampire…

It was a few years before I'd met my wife and

rejoined my fist. Quite a while before my name and likeness were plastered on notice boards featuring ridiculous amounts of gold being offered for my head.

The five of us had just entered the sleepy little hamlet of Hindal. We'd been hired by the local lord to investigate the town. Reports had been coming in that merchants that entered the town didn't come out the other end like they were supposed to.

Hatch, our fearless leader, figured it out right away. It was actually pretty simple if you gave it any thought. We walked into town in the middle of the day and saw nobody. No movement at windows, no dogs begging for scraps at street corners, and no birdsong filling the air.

We had to confirm his theory, though, so we kicked open the locked door to the inn and found the rooms full of the missing merchants.

They were packed in fairly tight. *Cheek to jowl* is the term I think you'd use.

They weren't breathing, but underneath the gray eyelids there was movement. Occasionally a leg twitched, like a dog chasing rabbits in its sleep.

At Hatch's signal I pulled the curtains away from the window and the room filled with sunlight.

Vampires really do burn when exposed to sunlight. Some legends about them are just bullshit, like the coffin thing, or the turning into swarms of bats. But the sunlight killing them is definitely true. Which is a good thing.

Hatch and I had to jump through the window to avoid the grasping hands. One followed us out into the sunlight, nothing but a vague shape wreathed in flames.

It took it a few steps before the fire died and a pile of ashes was all that was left.

We spent the rest of the day, using every minute of daylight, moving from home to home. Some were empty, some held more rooms of unbreathing, dreaming monsters. We burned all of them.

The final house was the mayor's manor.

"They're cocky sons of bitches," Hatch explained to me. This had been my first time facing the things, after all. "One'll move in, decide he likes a town and make himself the lord, turn or eat everyone else. Sometimes they just make thralls, though I hear that's harder than just turning."

"Thralls?" I asked.

"Yeah. Keeps the locals alive, but messes with their minds so they would do anything for the sucker. The smarter, more powerful ones usually do that. Then they can hide longer. And they have an unlimited food supply."

I then asked a question that might have sounded stupid, but early on Hatch had told me that there were no stupid questions in monster-hunting. Not knowing something could get you killed. "Is sunlight and fire the only way to kill them?"

He shook his head. "Nah. But they're a damn sight easier than any of the other methods."

"What are they?" I asked. In that world, Bram Stoker had never written the instruction manual.

"Wooden stake through the heart. Water blessed by a priest. Not any priest, mind. Has to have been a priest of whatever god the sucker worshipped before being turned, so don't worry about that one. Also, the stake only works if you cut off the head right away and bury the body and head in different graves. So, fire and sunlight are really the best options."

"What if you burn the body after you stake it?" I asked.

Hatch considered. "Probably'd work. But the important bit is that they're cocky, alright? Remember that. Once they're established they're too sure of themselves to ever move. Makes them easier to kill. They're so much more powerful than us mere mortals that they never stop to consider that maybe, just maybe, we actually know how to kill them."

After our short lesson, we'd ventured into the manor.

It hadn't taken long to find the vampire. It was just as Hatch had said. It was in the master bedroom. The thick curtains were closed against the sun, but the monster just lay on the large four-post bed. We could see her through the thin curtains that ran around the bed.

As we stepped inside the room it shifted. The curtains of the bed parted and the vampire stood, considering us.

She was beautiful. I don't mind admitting that. I was young and full of hormones. I wanted to do things to her body other than setting it on fire.

But I was a professional. So instead I was punched in the gut and sent flying through a wooden wall.

I could hear the others fighting as I struggled to my feet. There was a scream, cut off by a sudden, wet sound.

I rushed into the room to find one of my comrades lying dead, minus a throat.

The beautiful creature turned to consider me again,

dark blood pouring down her torso, causing the thin nightgown to cling in ways that made me hate myself.

Her momentary distraction at my reentrance was enough for Hatch to rip a curtain away from a window. The light of the sun stopped just shy of the vampire.

She laughed as the two other surviving members of the team tore down the other curtains. None of the sunlight reached her.

The other three stood within the squares of light, though, and all looked to me. It was the look you give a cow you'd been particularly fond of right before sending it to the butcher.

She studied them and the sunlight, the *fading* sunlight, before turning back to me as I stood in the shadowed hole in the wall.

Sun. It's the easiest way to kill a vampire. Fire if the sun's not around. And if you can't bring the sun to a vampire, you take the vampire to the sun.

She blinked in surprise as I charged forward, my most ferocious war cry ripping from my throat.

Vampires are fast, but you can still catch them by surprise if you try hard enough. Apparently this one had never been tackled before.

I was able to lift her feet off the ground and carry her the three steps into the nearest square of light.

She began to scream and thrash almost instantly, and a sudden rush of flame caused me to throw myself away from her.

The four of us stood around her, weapons ready, until the fire stopped. Then we burned the manor down and left Hindal as nothing but a memory.

We were not paid nearly enough for the job.

SEVEN

I DID manage to get a few hours of sleep. I'd finally risked sneaking into the room and passing out on the bed beside Pat.

She was gone and the bedroom door was sitting open when I came to. I was shaken out of sleep by the sound of Garack and Lukill shouting something about the show they were watching.

I groaned and rolled to a sitting position. I sat in a contemplative silence for a while. I considered a lot of things. Leaving town; reporting the vampires to the authorities; calling the wizard Jackson.

In the end I decided I was in need of a hobby.

I performed all the various required rituals in the apartment's tiny bathroom, then greeted my family. Garack—we had decided we were going to start calling him Jack so he'd fit in better—spent a few breathless minutes telling me about the hero of the show he and his cousin were watching.

I pretended to listen and nodded my head and "oo-ed" and "ah-ed" at the appropriate moments.

When he was done I kissed Pat good morning. "I just have to make a quick phone call, then I'm heading out for the day."

She gave me a questioning look and I whispered in her ear. "There's a possible problem. I'm going to deal with it."

She nodded her understanding and wished me luck.

We didn't have a phone in the apartment so I made my way to the street and stuck a quarter in the payphone that rested under the one streetlight that managed to turn on every night.

It rang a few times before a woman's voice answered. "Hello, Cochran Construction."

"Is this Sylvia?" I asked, making my voice as friendly as possible.

"It is. I recognize that voice. How are you doing, Gary?" Her tone changed from bored to friendly.

"Doing great, Syv. Hey, Larry's not around, is he?"

"No, I'm sorry, he's at a site all morning."

"No problem. Maybe you can help me then?" I asked.

"I can certainly try."

"You wouldn't happen to know which motel Larry has his out-of-town crews use, do you?"

"I do. You needing a night away from the wife and kids, Gary?"

I laughed. "Something like that. So what's this place called?"

"It's the Sunside Motel. It's on the east end of town, just off the freeway." She gave me a rough approximation of the address.

"Thanks, Sylvia. You're my hero. Tell Larry I say hi

when you see him."

I hung up and made my way to my car.

The Sunside was easy to find. The big, fading sign was visible from the freeway and it wasn't even a block away from the exit.

The place was exactly what I'm sure you're already imagining: a U-shaped, single-story building with lines of faded doors and large windows all facing the parking lot. A large sign proudly proclaimed "Cable TV and Pool."

The parking lot was sparse. Only three cars rested between any of the faded lines, and I assumed at least one of them belonged to whoever ran the place.

I parked in front of the office and made my way inside.

Behind the built-in desk sat a short man with messy hair and a pair of sharp, pointed ears.

"Can I help you?" he asked without looking up from the magazine resting in his lap.

"Any chance you're related to Ben Peck?" I asked the gnome.

He looked up sharply. "Why, cause I'm short?" His anger dissipated a little when he saw who had asked the question. I have that effect on people.

"No, cause you're a gnome, and I was under the impression that the Peck family had that market cornered." I put on my best friendly smile.

He actually smiled back, which was a good sign, I thought. "Yeah. He's actually my brother. And I'm guessing you're related to Kaga Bloodfist."

"My brother."

"Alright, so we both have famous brothers."

"They may be famous, but they sure didn't get the looks."

"Damn straight." He closed his magazine and stood up on his chair, extending a hand. "Name's Mitchell."

"Gary." I enveloped his tiny hand in my own and we both pretended it wasn't ridiculous.

"What can I do for you, Gary?"

"This might sound weird, but I was actually hoping you could tell me about the group of men that went missing a few nights ago."

"The construction guys?"

"Yeah."

He shrugged. "Not much to tell, really. They'd reserved two rooms for the week. Day two they just vanished. Both rooms were trashed. Maid found some blood in one of them. Why you asking?"

I shook my head. "No real reason beyond an unhealthy need to know everybody's business. Anyone else go missing like that?"

He looked uncomfortable at that question but he answered anyway. "You see the news reports about that girl that went missing?"

I nodded.

"Yeah, well, she was on her way back up to Morgantown for school. She'd stopped here for a night. Next morning her room was empty and the car was still in the parking lot."

"Shit."

"Tell me about it. Luckily most of our business comes from people just passing through and being too tired to keep going, otherwise we'd be in real trouble."

"I'm sure. Where I'm from that sort of reputation

would really cause problems."

"Where *are* you from? Kaga's never told me. With the accent I'd guess Eastern Europe or something."

I just grinned. "Not important. Anyway, how much is it for a room?"

He stared at me. "What?"

"Wife kicked me out. Too many late nights drinking with my brother."

Pat never would have kicked me out for that. Compared to goblins, orcs are damn well behaved when drinking. Although, I didn't think she'd argue at the prospect of having one less body in the apartment for a few days.

Six people disappearing from a location in such a short amount of time was too much of a coincidence for me. Plus, I already knew we had vampires in Summervale. It was incredibly likely they were here.

Like Hatch had taught me, they're too full of themselves to even consider that staying in one place was dangerous for them.

That's not to say they wouldn't leave if they knew they were found out and didn't think they could handle the situation, but I was confident that they hadn't moved on yet.

Mitchell gave me a price and I prepaid for three nights.

Another thing about vampires that is actually true: They have to be invited into your home. If you've paid for a room, you're living there. Even if it's not actually your home, the vampire can't differentiate. They need an invite. So I was going to set up shop and watch for them from the safety of a hopefully comfortable bed.

EIGHT

THE FIRST THING you need to do before you start a hunt of any kind is get supplies. Figure out what you're up against and what you're going to need to make sure the fight is as one-sided as possible.

Of course, if you listen to my old buddy Hatch, you would be under the impression that the first thing you'd need to do is give a quote and get half your payment up front.

That's all well and good if there's a noble of some kind willing to foot the bill, but this world isn't really big on that sort of thing.

In fact, I was pretty sure that if I reported the vampires to the authorities, nothing would be done.

That elf woman would ask for evidence, I'd show her the three men, now vampires, that had showed up at the Bearded Lady, and all that would happen would be a celebration. They'd rescued three of the five missing men, and even found the horrible monster—me— responsible for their disappearance.

I'd likely then be questioned about the girl that had

disappeared. Some sort of evidence would be planted and I would find myself locked up.

Okay, okay, I know. That's all paranoia. But you have to bear in mind that I grew up in a world where being an orc meant you had a *Guilty* sign hanging around your neck. Sure, more often than not I *had* been guilty, but that was because it was better to actually reap the reward of the crime before the punishment, rather than just the punishment.

And we'd all be lying if we said there weren't problems like that on this world, too.

Anyway, the point was, whether I reported the vampires or not, there wasn't likely going to be any sort of reward in it for me, so I figured I might as well do something about them.

For the sake of the community. Not because I have some sort of irrational bloodlust or anything.

I left the Sunside motel and made my way back into Summervale proper.

My first stop was the apartment. I told Pat what I had learned and she listened impassively as I told her my plan. In the end she just shrugged. "Let me know if you need any help."

I then changed into my best suit. My weekly poker games with the guys had taught me the importance of dressing the part. Especially if you were going to be talking business. And I had decided that killing vampires was a profession, not a hobby.

I left the apartment and made my way to the little office building where Ben Peck ran all his various endeavors. I might not be able to get anything from the authorities for this, but Ben would likely want to hear about any issues with his property.

Five mailboxes sat outside the front door, each proclaiming the name of the companies that called the building home. The one in the middle, claiming Suite 3, was for Peck Holdings.

I entered the building and headed to the second story for Suite 3.

Ben's niece, Moira, sat behind the receptionist's desk. She looked up from the magazine she was reading and considered me. She didn't ask anything, just waited for me to speak.

"I'm here to see Ben."

She nodded like she'd been expecting that. "He's in his office, go ahead."

I didn't question that maybe he'd like some warning before I marched in, but I only had so much daylight left to get everything checked off my list.

He looked up from the green text on his screen and stared at me as I entered.

"Gary?"

"Sorry to drop in unannounced like this, but I need to talk to you about something."

"Okay. Please, have a seat." He indicated one of two empty seats in front of his desk.

I closed the door and sat down. "What do you know about vampires?" I asked.

He blinked and opened and closed his mouth a few times before saying anything. "You're being serious, aren't you?"

I nodded. "I think you've got one in your motel. At least a few fresh-made, too."

"Which motel?"

"The Sunside."

He furrowed his brows for a moment before realization dawned. "You're sure?"

"Remember that crew that went missing from there?"

He nodded.

"I ran into them at the Bearded Lady last night. I've fought vampires before. I know the signs."

"I heard about that. Kaga told me." He considered for a while before speaking again. "But you're sure about the Sunside?"

I nodded. "They don't like to move around much once they find somewhere they like. I'm willing to bet a steady stream of people most of the locals wouldn't miss would make the Sunside very appealing."

He leaned back in his chair. "I need to tell Mitchell." He leaned forward, reaching for his phone.

I placed a hand on the phone and pushed it gently back into the cradle. "I wouldn't."

"Why not?" he demanded.

"I'd be willing to bet he's been enthralled. I stopped by there this morning. He seemed fine, but I wouldn't risk it. You tell him you know, he tells them we know. They leave town."

"What are you saying, Gary?"

I'd been planning on just killing the suckers for something to do, but Hatch's training was resurfacing.

I kept my face impassive as I spoke. "I'm assuming you have a budget for exterminators?"

It took less effort than I'd expected to convince Ben to pay for my services. I realized later that I'd set my price far too low.

After completing that step in the process, I took my advance of the payment and made my way to the one place I was fairly certain I could get any supplies I might need.

Danyl Ironbeard, owner of the Bearded Lady, also owned one of two pawn shops in Summervale.

His shop had become popular in the past year with my orc and goblin family. They were constantly stopping in to sell some trinket from the old world for rent or beer money. Those that had jobs even bought things back from him occasionally.

I went there now because he'd known how to chase off the monsters from the bar. He was a dwarf, which meant if he was anything like the dwarves back home, he was going to have weaponry that would be more effective against my targets than a gun. Although, I also planned on getting one of those.

Danyl Ironbeard ran the DI Pawn and Loan during the day, and mostly left the management of the bar to his wife, Kide, though they both spent their evenings at the bar. They'd turned down any offer of help when I'd suggested a few members of the goblin horde as barkeepers or cooks—the little bastards are surprisingly adept with that sort of work. The couple apparently just liked working.

Danyl greeted me as I entered the store, bell jingling to announce my arrival.

"Well, if it isn't my hero. What can I do for you, Gary?" Danyl asked.

I grinned as I approached the counter. "Well, I was hoping you might happen to have or at least know where I could find a few items."

"Oh, that's what I do. What're you looking for?"

"I need some holy symbols, blessed water, something sharp enough to sever a spinal cord, and a gun if you have one."

He stared for a moment. "Holy shit, you're going after the vampires from last night, aren't you?"

I nodded. "I think I found where they're holed up. Got the okay from the owner to clear them out."

Danyl looked impressed. "And you actually want to go after them?"

I shrugged. "It's paid work. Why not?"

He shook his head and let out a small laugh. "Alright. Well, holy symbols are easy. You're gonna want crosses. The three from last night were obviously Christian, based on how they ran away from Kide's cross. Here." He slid open a drawer and dug around inside for a minute before producing a small silver cross. "Then holy water? I don't carry that. I think you might be able to convince any of the holy men around town to help with that one. You've got a decent selection of reverends, preachers, priests. You name it, we probably have it. At least the Christian variety. Last two are doable as well. As far as sharp goes, what's your preference?"

"Always been better with axes, but a good heavy blade will work too."

"I have an axe. Should work. I'll sharpen it up for you, too." He disappeared into a back room and came back with a single-bladed axe obviously made for chopping wood. "What do you think?" He held it up for me to inspect.

I nodded. "Should do just fine. And the gun?" I had

no experience with guns beyond what I'd seen on television, but I'd always wanted one.

"Anything specific you're after?" He pulled a ring of keys out of a pocket and unlocked a metal cabinet. Inside were shelves of weapons.

"Something easy to shoot. Easy to carry without being seen."

"Conceal carry. Sure, sure. Got your license for that?" I returned his question with a blank expression.

His grin widened. "Of course, of course you do. How silly of me." He reached into the cabinet and pulled a small gun off the shelf.

I knew very little about guns, but I'd seen similar weapons on TV before. It was a revolver.

"This is a .38 special. This little guy used to be a service piece. Bought it off the local precinct when they upgraded a few years ago." He stopped and considered the gun before putting it back on the shelf. "You don't want that one. You want this one."

He pulled out an identical revolver and set it on the counter.

"What's the difference?" I asked.

"The difference is, if you shoot someone with this one, the cops don't trace it back to me."

"You're assuming I'm going to shoot someone?"

He didn't say anything for a long minute. Just met my eyes. Neither of us blinked.

Finally he shrugged. "I wouldn't dare accuse you something like that, Gary."

"Good. So how much for all of it?"

We agreed on a price fairly quickly. Cost me most of

Ben's advance, but Danyl was kind enough to throw in a box of ammunition and the cross necklace for free.

"Thanks, Danyl." I rested the axe over my left shoulder and shook the dwarf's hand.

"Anytime, Gary. Let me know how it goes. And if you need anything else before the job's done."

I really appreciated the fact that he pretended like he didn't think I was going to die.

NINE

THE ROOM WASN'T the worst I'd ever stayed in. Compared to some of the inns I've seen, the Sunside is downright swanky. But its real selling point was the fact that I had a room almost as large as my apartment to myself. No little orcs taking up the floor with their pillow and blanket nests, no irritable sister occupying the couch along with the remains of her last trip to the liquor store, and no weird smell coming up from the kitchen sink.

"We need to move," I murmured to myself as I turned my attention back to the window and my surveillance of my fellow guests.

The parking lot had filled a little since I'd first arrived. There were six cars in the lot beside my own and Mitchell's. I watched as the guests went from their rooms to the pool, or into town and back with conspicuous brown paper bags. All lit by the neon sign and a few street lamps.

There was at least one other guest that had been there before me, as far as I could tell.

The redhead attracted the eye in the same way gold attracts dragons. That's a lot, if you weren't sure. It was as irresistible a pull as any body has had on a pair of eyes.

She rounded the corner from the pool and walked past my window where I sat watching the doors.

I assumed there was a swimsuit under the towel, but I let my imagination do its thing.

And before anyone says anything, yes, I am a happily married man. But I was sitting in a dark motel room, alone, spying on my neighbors. It was the perfect scenario to let my mind wander.

I followed the swaying figure along the length of one wall's worth of doors, and fully intended to watch her progress the entire way to her room. She was the only guest I hadn't seen before, and I wanted to make sure I knew which room she was in—for vampire-hunting purposes.

She passed an open room door. Standing inside was another young woman nervously standing with arms crossed in front of her and a young man in a blue hat talking to her. He seemed to be trying to talk his way into the room.

I ignored the two of them for a moment as I continued to watch the redheaded woman, but the man turned his head to watch her come, then turned the other way after she passed to watch her leave.

I forgot about the towel-clad woman instantly.

The hat had a confederate flag on the front. I recognized the face as well.

I'd found one of my vampires.

As I made my way into the warm night air, the young

50

woman had stepped aside and confederate-hat was slinking into the room.

I shouldered my axe and cut across the parking lot toward the closing door.

I made it right before the latch clicked. I didn't think it was a good time for niceties, what with the murderous baby vampire about to do what vampires do, so I placed my hand on the door and pushed it open.

"What the—?" the girl began.

"Sorry, miss, this won't take long." I pushed past her into the room and strode toward Confederate Hat. I really wished I'd bothered to learn his name so I could call him something else. But it was probably for the best. If all I had to go on was his apparent attachment to that particular piece of Earth's history, it would probably make it easier to kill him.

Not that I would have felt too bad about it either way.

The man had been admiring the room—which was identical to all the others—as I'd stepped inside. He turned to face me, a look of confusion sprouting on his face right before I swung the axe.

The blade cut through his shoulder and lodged itself in bone. Black, acrid blood sprayed out and painted one wall.

The vampire screamed and jerked away from me, pulling the axe out of my hands.

I staggered forward from the sudden movement and met the vampire's fist mid step.

He hit me on the right side of my face and sent me flying across the room. My feet barely registered the floor before I smashed into the room's small wooden table.

The table reacted in the normal fashion for when a three-hundred-pound orc is thrown across a room to land on it. It broke.

I staggered to my feet, hand grasping around my throat for the cross necklace. And it wasn't there.

I had a sudden image in my mind of the thin silver chain resting on the table in my room.

Luckily, I still had a plan B. I pulled the small plastic bottle out of a pocket and turned to face the vampire.

He had just pulled the axe out of his shoulder, another spurt of blood accompanying the blade on its exit.

The room's tenant was huddled in the corner. She seemed too shocked to even be able to manage a scream.

I quickly unscrewed the bottle top, then rushed forward before the vampire could pick which one of us to kill first.

He spun to face me as I made his decision for him, raising my axe above his head.

I flung the bottle out toward him. The clear water sailed through the air and struck him in the face.

Nothing happened.

We stood in silence for a moment. I stood, arm extended, legs spread in a fighting stance, and empty plastic bottle held like a rapier aimed at his face.

He stood, face dripping with water and axe raised for a killing blow.

After what was likely longer than I had any right to still be alive, I spoke. "You're not Baptist, are you?"

He screwed up his face in confusion before letting out a cry and swinging the axe down toward me.

I managed to jump back out of the way. I took another step back as he advanced toward me. Then another. The last step ended with me tripping over a pile of the kindling that had been a table.

The confederate vampire smiled down at me, his eyes again filling with that unnatural red.

I searched desperately for a solution, and grabbed the nearest thing to a weapon I could find: a table leg.

I swung the improvised weapon, and the jagged edge caught him just above the knee and ripped away denim and flesh.

He grunted in pain from the blow before he brought the axe down again.

I managed to roll out of the way and hurry to my feet as he struggled to pull the blade out of the floor. It was not a graceful rise, but I thank any gods that might be that it was fast.

As the vampire finally pried the axe loose, he spun to face me.

I timed it as well as I could. I waited until his chest was at the right angle, then I hurriedly stepped in close and thrust the jagged edge of the table leg up.

There was some cracking as the wood broke, but I kept pushing. Soon the cracking wood was replaced with cracking ribs, and then the sound of blood on carpet, then a gasp of pain, then nothing.

The vampire slumped forward, full weight resting on my right arm and the makeshift stake.

"You killed him."

I'd almost forgotten about the woman.

I turned to face her and she was curled up in the corner of the room, trying to push herself into the wall to get away from me.

"Not quite yet. You're welcome, by the way."

She didn't seem to register what I was saying. Which might have been for the best.

I dropped the vampire to the ground. The stake hit first and propped him up for a second before slowly tilting to drop him on his side. I crossed the room to the bed, where on the bedside table sat a phone.

I grabbed the phone cord and ripped it out of the wall. Didn't need her calling the cops.

If I was lucky, none of the neighbors would either. There had been a bit of noise in that fight.

I then ripped the bed's thin blanket off and returned to the vampire. I laid the blanket out and threw him on top of it.

After I'd wrapped him up, I threw him over my shoulder and picked up my axe.

I made my way to the exit. "Lock this door and don't let anybody else in."

I made sure to close the door behind me as I left. There was the click of the deadbolt and chain almost immediately.

TEN

MY CAR WAS PARKED in the farthest spot on the lot. The room it stood in front of was unoccupied from what I could tell, so I figured it was as safe a spot as any for the next bit.

I unrolled the blanket on the other side of my car, hopefully obscuring the sight of what I was about to do from the rest of the motel.

I brought the axe down. It took a few swings, but I managed to remove the head.

I had a cooler in the back of the car, and I dropped the head in there. I rewrapped the body in the blanket and dropped it in the trunk. I would throw it in the sun somewhere the next day, let that take care of it. If I shined a little sunlight in the trunk and the cooler, it should take care of any lingering blood, as well. I hoped it would, anyway.

One down.

I headed back to my room with a feeling of accomplishment.

"That's a nice big axe you have there."

I froze at the voice. The sound of it wrapped itself around my mind and stroked gently. I shivered as I turned to face the woman.

It was the redhead. She was still wrapped in her towel from the pool. She swayed toward me, the towel falling to the ground. She apparently had been skinny dipping.

She smiled at my choked response and swaggered closer.

Every instinct was telling me to run. This was it, this was the vampire that had created the others. I knew it without needing proof.

Although, my inability to move was probably proof enough. I could feel the gentle hand as it slowly wrapped around my mind. Could feel her will exerting itself over my own.

She was only a few steps away now. I knew I needed to run. Needed to get to the safety of my room. Or at least swing the axe. Maybe I'd get lucky and take off her head. But I didn't want to. Her hold on me was such that I just stood there, axe gripped uselessly in shaking hands.

I was able to move when she touched me. It was just an involuntary shudder as her hand trailed a slow, ponderous path down my chest.

She reached up with her other hand and ran it through my hair. At the back of my head she balled it into a fist, grabbing a handful of hair. It hurt, in the best possible way.

She pulled my face down toward her own.

I watched with fascinated horror as the whites of her eyes slowly filled with red, the crimson spilling over to cover the blue. Two perfectly red almonds stared up at me as she pulled my mouth to her own.

The kiss would have been good if not for the taste of blood. She had fed recently and her mouth was still thick with it.

That was apparently all I needed to shake myself free of her control—the thought of someone else's lifeblood pouring down her bare chest. I almost threw up in her mouth.

She pulled back and studied me, head cocked to the side in confusion. I didn't give her time to react beyond that.

I brought the axe up and into her belly.

She let out a shocked gasp and released me. She took a step back and stared down at the black liquid pouring out of her and onto the asphalt.

I stumbled back as she released me, leaving the axe in her gut, and shook my head, trying to loose the last of the invisible fingers wrapped around my mind.

She looked up and gave me a feral grin. "I was hoping we could have some fun before this part."

Her skin began to twitch and shift, as though there were something moving just under the surface. Something that wanted to get out.

It got out.

There was a tearing sound as the transformation started. Skin peeled away from her face as her jaw elongated, her canine teeth extending well beyond a point that was natural, and every other tooth in her mouth shifted and grew, until an army of sharp teeth smiled down at me.

And it was *down* at me. As her face had changed, so had the rest of her. Arms extended and fingers lengthened, growing talons longer even than her teeth. Leathery wings unfolded from the arms.

Her legs grew and her knees reversed as extra joints fell into place. She stood well over ten feet tall before she fell forward onto all fours, and she still towered over me.

Her torso ripped open, revealing a mass of black leather and muscles that rippled and shifted with every movement.

A massive black mane of fur filled out her figure and she shook, like Hell's worst dog, shimmering blackness shifting in the yellow light of the motel's parking lot.

My axe clattered to the ground as the wound in her stomach knit itself shut.

I managed an "Oh shit," before eyes so dark a red that they might be mistaken for black locked onto me.

Her mouth opened and she screamed. It sounded like a thousand bats trying to claw their way through my ears.

Again I found myself unable to move. No invisible battle of wills this time, just pure, concentrated fear.

I'd seen vampires transform before. It happened a lot, but usually it was only after I'd set them on fire. I'd never witnessed one in perfect health do this trick. It was one of the most horrible things I'd ever watched. And I've seen some shit, let me tell you.

She took a slow, purposeful step toward me, horrible

face leaning down to eye level. The wall of teeth widened as the monster grinned at me.

I thought about those teeth closing over my throat and I was able to find movement again.

My new gun was in my hand and pointed at the thing's face before I knew what I was doing.

The smile vanished instantly as the six slugs punched her splintering teeth into the back of her skull.

The sound of a thousand bats screaming in pain drowned out the echo of the gunshots.

I turned to run but a massive taloned hand caught me in the side and I sailed across the sidewalk in front of the rooms and through the glass of the end room.

I almost landed on the bed. It still would have hurt even if I had.

I rolled over and gasped in pain as I pushed myself to my feet. Blood poured out of my side where massive claws had caught me, and from countless other small cuts from the glass.

I didn't have time to check for any potentially life-threatening injuries as I felt a foot press on my back and push.

I flew through another wall and slid to a stop against the room's bathtub.

I groaned as I tried to find the strength to do something beyond just lie on the floor and hurt.

A strong hand, thankfully human-shaped, grabbed my shoulder and flipped me over onto my back.

She looked human again, though her eyes were still red. She leaned down, her horrifyingly beautiful face twisted into a malicious grin. A grin I was disappointed to see had all its teeth.

"Come on, big boy, you must have more spirit than that. I can only enjoy a meal if I work up a sweat first." Her long red hair fell down around her face and rested in a downy pile next to my head. "And we don't have to fight. I have other ways of wearing myself out."

A claw-tipped finger traced a pattern on my chest, cutting through shirt and skin like paper.

I bared my tusks at her. "Go to hell."

With a burst of adrenaline-fueled speed I grabbed a fistful of her soft, bright hair and pulled her down. I threw the top of my head into her nose.

It felt like I'd head-butted a cement wall, but her face was thrown back, dark blood streaming.

As she staggered back I managed to get to my feet. I threw both hands into the mass of red locks and grabbed as much as I could.

She was most certainly stronger than I was, but she still weighed almost nothing in her human form. With less effort than I'd expected, I was able to swing.

She let out a surprised cry as her feet left the ground.

Her bent knees scraped the ceiling as I swung her over my head and brought her down with a loud crunch over the side of the faded pink bathtub. She grunted in pain, doubled over and grasping at where her stomach had smashed the tub's rim.

I didn't give her any time to react and just kept swinging. I spun her around to the side, and her backside connected with the toilet—pink to match the tub—shattering the tank in a shower of cheap porcelain and water.

I prepared to swing again but stumbled back with

fistfuls of hair. I stared down in surprise as the smooth red began to turn gray and crumble in my hand.

I looked up to find the woman's skin writhing again. This time she started growing before her skin peeled away.

I didn't waste time watching the transformation. Watching that once was more than enough for any lifetime.

I lost precious seconds unlocking the door, and regretted not just jumping back out through the window.

I was two doors down when the wall around the open door erupted in a hail of drywall and insulation.

The monster let out its thousand-bat cry and came loping after me.

Luckily I'm not a total idiot and had left my room's door unlocked. I had anticipated the possibility of having to make a hasty retreat.

I turned the knob and fell into my room. I spun and crab-crawled backward away from the door, pulling my feet over the threshold just as the monster snapped its jaws over the spot.

It spat out the concrete it had taken with the bite and turned to consider me.

A talon-tipped hand reached out and stopped when it hit the threshold. It flattened out as though it were pressing against glass, then it pulled away.

The creature sighed and there was a shimmering in the air, and the thing in the doorway seemed to dissolve into a wall of ash that was swept away by a non-existent wind to reveal the beautiful, naked woman from before.

"Come on. Do you really think you have a chance against me?" She leaned against the wall and ran a finger up and down along the door frame. "I'm almost a hundred and fifty, you know. We just get stronger with age. With every drop of blood we drink."

"I know," I said, as I slowly pushed myself to my feet. "Killed a few of you in my time."

Her eyes narrowed, and then she smiled. "I believe that. I haven't been hurt like this in a while. Not that you've done any real damage, but still. You've put up a fight."

"How's this then?" I grabbed the thin silver chain from the room's table and dangled it in front of her face.

She spared it a glance before rolling her eyes. She pushed herself away from the wall and stood in the center of the door again, arms folded beneath her breasts. "Oh, please. You know it only works if that symbol meant anything to us in life, right?"

I deflated. "I was told everyone around here was Christian." I gave her an apologetic smile. "Sorry."

She laughed. "Don't apologize. I was Christian, though many argued that point. Mormon, you see. They don't revere the cross as a symbol like most. Never has had an effect on me."

She turned again, resting her back against the wall and looking at me over her shoulder. She bit her lip and looked up at me. "You know, I bet you'd have fun as a vampire. You're already so big and strong. What d'you say?"

"Sorry. Happily married." I closed the door before she could say anything else.

I leaned up against the door and peered through the viewer. She gave a dramatic sigh, and pushed herself away from the wall. "I'll be back, killer, don't worry."

She stood on her tiptoes and peered in through the hole. "And I don't think I want to kill you. I want you with me." She grinned wickedly as she sauntered away.

I watched her go, but only to make sure she really was gone, I swear. Then I collapsed onto the bed. I didn't worry about my blood as it stained the blanket.

ELEVEN

HE CAME a little sooner than I had expected. There was the click of the deadbolt sliding open, and the door swung in.

The chain did its job and stopped the door.

I could have pushed the door back closed at this point, but I waited patiently as the bolt cutters slid in through the gap from below and cut the chain.

I was a little impressed. It was almost silent. The cutters and the chain made much less noise than I'd expected. I had a suspicion that Mitchell had done this before.

I stood just to the side of the door, between it and the large window, and waited as the door slowly creaked open.

Once it was open enough I didn't wait for the gnome to enter on his own. I reached out and wrapped my large hands around his small head and yanked him inside.

He gave out a cry as I did so, but I threw a hand over his mouth. He struggled against me, but I had every advantage in this fight.

At least, I thought I did. He stabbed my arm with the room key he was still holding.

More out of surprise than pain I loosened my grip and he shouted out, "Come in."

I decided I didn't care about being nice and smashed his head against the wall. He went limp immediately.

I threw him onto the bed and spun to the door expecting the redhead. Instead another familiar face stepped inside.

A young man with a burn mark grinned at me, his white teeth glowing softly in the dark of the room.

"Just you?" I asked the construction worker-turned-vampire.

"All we need," he said, stepping inside.

"That is great to hear."

I didn't have my axe anymore, but I did have a pocket knife that I made sure to always keep with me. It had been enough to carve a few stakes out of the wooden furniture in the room.

I pulled the improved chair leg out from my waistband and rammed it through the man's chest.

His eyes opened wide in surprise and he fell in a heap on the floor.

"Gods, but I love you baby vamps," I said to his dead eyes as I dragged him inside the room. "Always so damn sure of yourselves. You think you're invincible. Makes you so easy to kill."

After I dumped the body in the bathtub, I tied up Mitchell and stuck him inside the room's closet with a sock stuffed inside his mouth and a strip of duct tape added just for safety.

I closed and relocked the door.

I sat on the bed, a row of carved stakes lined up next to me, and prepared for the long wait until morning.

It was less than an hour later that the window shattered. The chair fell on the floor in front of me and I looked up as a young woman attempted to climb over the sharp glass. It was the same girl I had rescued from Confederate Hat. I guess she hadn't taken my advice.

I took the few steps across the room and picked her up before she could cut herself anymore on the shards of glass still standing in the frame.

I held a hand over her mouth and wrapped my other arm around her throat until she stopped struggling.

I gently laid her down on the bed and did my best to bandage the cuts she'd given herself from attempting to crawl over the glass.

"I can do this all night, you know." The redhead rested an arm on the frame and grinned in at me.

I was relieved to see she had decided to dress herself for this visit.

I nodded my head toward her. "So can I."

She let out a little moan and closed her eyes. "Oh, I know you can. God, but you need to just let me in." Her voice was deep and hungry. "Please?"

When she opened her eyes they were the regular blue, not the deep red.

"Sorry, can't do that."

She let out a sigh and gave me a long look, her eyes moving up and down as she studied me. "We could have so much fun together."

"Well," I said as I gently tied up the girl and taped her mouth shut. "I don't know about you, but I'm having more fun than I've had in a while."

I put the girl in the closet next to Mitchell and turned to face the woman in the window.

Her grin showed a little more tooth. "I'm having a blast."

"You know this only ends with one of us dead, right?" I said.

She shrugged. "I've been dead for over a hundred years, killer. I'm really good at it."

I considered her. I'd never spoken to a vampire before. It made the thought that I had to kill her less appealing. "Why do you do it?" I asked, finally.

"Do what?"

"Kill people. Turn them. The whole bit."

She gave me a look like I was an idiot. "I have to. I have no choice in the matter. Besides, it's just so much fun."

"How many people have you killed?" I asked. Her callous statement about it being fun had helped remind me that she was a monster. A monster with a beautiful mask, but still a monster.

Her grin tweaked itself into a crueler line. "How many cows have you caused to be slaughtered? How many ants have you stepped on? That's a ridiculous question and you know it."

I nodded. "Thank you."

She cocked her head to the side at my response. "For what? Are you accepting my offer?"

"I just wanted to thank you."

"Oh?"

"Yes. Would you like to come inside?" I asked.

Her grin grew. "Really?"

I nodded. "Is your offer still on the table? Of wearing yourself out first?"

I undid my tie and dropped it to the floor.

"For you? Of course." In a fluid motion she was standing on the window sill and then on the glass-strewn carpet.

She was wearing a loose-fitting tank top and a pair of jean shorts that showed more than they hid as she walked slowly across the room, glass crunching under her bare feet.

Her eyes moved up and down my body as I undid the buttons on my shirt.

"You're serious?" she asked, stopping in front of me.

I shrugged out of my shirt and nodded. "I don't want to die with any regrets."

"What happened to happily married?"

I sighed. "Happily might have been an exaggeration."

Her grin widened as she slowly reached out and began to undo my belt.

"Hang on." I placed a hand over hers.

She looked up, eyes red again, full of hunger. "What?"

"You first."

"Whatever you say." She bit her lip again as she grasped her shirt with both hands and began to pull it up over her head.

I watched as the shirt moved up, revealing the same smooth stomach, the heavy, pale breasts tipped with caramel.

It was harder to do than I had expected. I almost

considered letting her finish first, but now was the best time.

While the shirt was still covering her face, I pulled another stake from my waistband and drove it through her chest.

She let out a sobbing cry. Her shirt dropped to reveal the look of betrayed pain on her face. "I thought…"

"Sorry." Part of me legitimately meant it, too.

Her face slacked, a look of resignation replacing the pain. "It's okay." A gentle hand came up and rested on my cheek as I gently laid her on the ground. "You know, it really could have been fun. Just the two of us." The red of her eyes faded away to show the blue.

"I think so, too. But it wouldn't have worked. Not in the long run."

"Not your type?" she asked, somehow managing a wry smile. "That's fair."

Then I pushed the stake in deeper and she fell still.

TWELVE

NIGHTS CAN BE LONG when you're waiting for morning. It can be longer when you're in pain and bleeding from multiple wounds.

I spent the night tearing sheets and rewrapping my bleeding cuts. None of them were serious, but they still stung whenever I moved. Especially the cuts from the vampire's massive talons.

When the sun finally broke over the horizon I dragged the body of the vampire—I almost regretted not learning her name—into the parking lot, stake still sticking out of her chest.

She caught flame immediately.

By the time I got back outside with the guy from my tub, her body was nothing but a pile of gray ash on the asphalt.

I dumped Confederate Hat's head out of the cooler after his body had already crumbled into gray dust. The hat burned long after the head had turned to ash and blown away.

After a quick trip to the nearest gas station I found a

pay phone. It rang a few times before a tired voice answered.

"Hello?"

"Ben, this is Gary."

"Gary? Do you have any idea what time it is?"

"Yeah. Hey, remember that issue we talked about yesterday? The extermination thing?"

He sounded more awake after that. "Yes?"

"I think it's mostly taken care of, but I want to be sure. What sort of insurance do you have on this place?"

"What?"

"You heard me."

"Damn it, Gary." He sighed. "Insurance would never cover an obvious fire. It's fine, I can rebuild without it if I need to. Just make sure you do it right."

"Yessir." I hung up and turned back to the Sunside Motel.

I dragged Mitchell and the girl out of my closet and propped them up against my car, which I'd parked across the street from the motel.

I left them tied up, just in case there was another mature vampire around to keep the control over them active.

I stole the keys off Mitchell's belt and made my way back to the motel.

I ignored the room with the smashed-out door. I'd already been able to confirm—against my will—that it was unoccupied. But I went to every other room.

I unlocked the first door and kicked it open, pulling the chain out of the door as I did so.

A couple sat up in their bed and screamed at the sight of the massive orc framed in the doorway.

"Wakeup call," I said, stepping aside and letting the sun past. It spread up the bed and over the couple.

After neither of them erupted into flames I stepped back out of the room. "You're going to want to pack up and leave as soon as possible." I didn't wait for them to leave before I returned with a large red gas can.

They hurried out very quickly after I started spilling gasoline around the room.

The next few rooms were empty, so I just poured some gas over the furniture and moved on.

I found the vampires in the next occupied room. They weren't in the beds, but were instead curled up inside the closet and in the tub of the bathroom.

The one in the bathtub I recognized from the picture of the construction crew and from the other night in the bar. I poured gasoline over him and he sat up with a choked cry.

"Morning," I said as I flicked a lighter and held the flame to his wrinkled shirt.

His screams woke the two vampires in the closet, and I watched as they rushed out the door and directly into the path of sunlight I had left for them by opening the curtains.

I stepped around the twitching mounds of flame and moved on the next room.

The few other human guests I found were quick to jump in their cars and leave without asking too many questions.

Same with the maids, just arriving for the early morning shift. I respectfully suggested that Mr. Peck would not mind at all if they just took the day off.

The last room in line was hers. I strode around the

room and inspected it. It was obvious she had been here for a while.

Old photographs hung on the walls, a collection of pictures of the red-haired woman in different time periods. Moving from an old black and white photo of her wearing a billowing dress with a collar that went up to her chin to one that appeared to have been cut from a magazine. It appeared my new friend had spent some time as a model. Not the kind that showed off clothes, though.

I pulled out the pin that held the picture to the wall and folded it to put it in my suit pocket.

I searched every corner of the room and found no other vampires.

Satisfied with my search, I covered every surface of her room with gasoline.

Then I dropped the matches.

I strode past every room I had doused—every other room held an empty gas can—and tossed in a lit match. The puddles on the floor lit up in lazy flames that spread from beds to chairs and up walls.

Once I was satisfied that the fire was burning well enough, I returned to my car and untied Mitchell and the young woman.

They both stirred and groaned awake. From the way they held their heads I guessed that being enthralled left one hell of a hangover.

"What happened?" the girl asked, looking around. Her face froze into a mask of terror when she saw me.

"It's okay." I did my best to appear non-threatening. "You might not remember everything that happened, but I promise, everything is okay now."

"You hit a man with an axe." She pointed accusingly at me. "But he didn't die…" Now she looked confused.

"I know, I was there. You might not believe it, but he was a vampire. I was trying to save you."

"Then the woman…" She didn't seem to be listening. She didn't seem to want to run away, either, so I left her to her reflections.

I turned to Mitchell, who was now standing next to the car and staring at the fire.

"My motel…"

"Sorry about the fire. It's kind of protocol with a vampire infestation."

"Vampire? Seriously?" He turned to me, but he didn't sound too disbelieving.

I nodded. "Yeah. Ben gave the okay to light the match. Just so you know."

Mitchell let out a laugh. "He would. Hopefully he doesn't bother rebuilding. You know, I hated running that place."

"Well, that makes me feel a little better."

In the distance sirens could be heard—the loud, deeper tone of a firetruck and the wail of police cruisers.

"What's the game plan?" Mitchell asked.

I shrugged. "If we're lucky that elf'll show up. She might believe me when I tell them I was killing vampires for your brother."

"Yeah. Won't hurt name-dropping Ben, either. We could just tell them he hired you to burn the place down for the insurance money and most of them would just accept it."

The flashing lights eventually made their way from the city and filled up the parking lot.

The firefighters worked quickly, setting up their perimeter and hooking their hoses to the hydrant.

I assured them no one was inside, but they still checked every room.

The EMTs sat the three of us—myself, Mitchell, and the young, now mute woman—on the edge of the ambulance.

I allowed them to bandage my chest with real gauze instead of just sheets and nodded my agreement that a trip to the hospital was a good idea.

The girl was fine except for some small cuts, but she agreed to being taken to the hospital as well.

Mitchell was told he had a concussion, which made me feel like a bit of a jerk.

Since none of us were in critical condition they drove all three of us in the same ambulance.

We sat in awkward silence the entire drive.

I was sitting on a paper-covered table when the detectives found me.

The elf, Detective Halldorson, stepped up to me and poked me in the chest. "I've been asking questions about you, orc."

"Ow." I put a hand to my freshly stitched wounds.

"And Mitchell Peck tells me you just burned his motel down to kill a vampire."

"Yeah, you're welcome." I gave my friendliest grin as her eyes opened wide in anger.

Her partner coughed politely. "Den, why don't you take a step back?"

She glared at him but did as he suggested. "I'm too old for this sort of bullshit, Matt," she grumbled as Fitzpatrick stepped up in front of me.

"Yeah yeah, whatever you say." He returned my smile. "We've already spoken to Mitchell and Ben Peck. Ben confirmed that he gave you the okay to light the fire. Which means the responsibility goes to him. He'll be fine, if you were worried. His name carries a lot of weight." He didn't sound super thrilled about that.

I nodded. "Sorry if I caused any trouble, but that's just what you do with vampires. Never know if one's hiding in the walls or something."

"No, that's not what you do." Denelle snorted. "Maybe in whatever backwater plane you crawled out of, but not here."

I stared at her for a moment. "You figured it out, huh?"

"What? That you're from another dimension? I'm an elf; different planes are what we do."

"I see."

"Can we stay on topic?" Matt asked.

"Of course." I turned back to him. "What do I need to do?"

"Just answer a couple questions for me. Corroborate what the Peck brothers told us. Then you can go."

Halldorson sighed. "Then you and I are having an unofficial talk about the correct way to deal with that sort of thing."

I blinked. "What do you mean?"

"Other than the unnecessary property damage, you killed a vampire. More than one, if my guess is right."

"At least six," I said.

She raised her eyebrows. "That's actually really impressive. But believe it or not, we actually have protocol for that sort of thing."

Matt sat down on the table next to me. "Damn. Have I ever told you, Den, that sometimes I really hate living in this town?"

"Yeah, you have."

"Why's that, Detective?" I asked.

"Well, for one, and no offense is meant to either of you, but I wouldn't mind living somewhere where my high school D&D campaign didn't shit on my real life."

"What's that?" I asked.

"Don't worry about that." Halldorson gave Fitzpatrick a look that meant they'd be talking later. "What does matter is that you need to promise to let me know the next time you decide to take on any monsters. If there's a chance for collateral damage, we need to be ready for it."

"That is much more reasonable than I expected, Detective."

"Much more reasonable than you deserve, too, but I got a phone call from a Mr. Smith this morning letting me know that I should be a little understanding of your situation. So maybe thank him next time you see him."

THIRTEEN

THE NEXT WEEK everything was almost back to normal. People around town talked about the fire, but no one seemed to know that I was the one that'd started it, and it appeared that Fitzpatrick and Halldorson had left out the V-word from their report.

Wednesday night came around and I met with the others for poker night.

This week we met in Larry's warehouse. We set the table in the middle of an aisle, surrounded by shelves of tools and boxes of nails and screws.

"So I hear you lost your motel." Larry puffed at his cigar as he adjusted the cards in his hand.

"I did." Ben's tone made it sound like he'd misplaced a pen rather than lost an entire building.

"Gonna rebuild?" Larry asked.

"Maybe."

"If you do, let me know. I can recommend a few guys that would be great for the job."

"Why don't you do it?" I asked.

Larry laughed. "Damn, Gary, I don't have the

manpower for that. Though, I gotta say, those two cousins of yours are pulling their weight. Hurck is a crew all on her own."

"Told you," I said.

Our conversation turned to other topics for a few hands before I brought it up again. "You know, Larry, I do have a lot of other cousins looking for work."

Larry looked at me over his cards. "Yeah?"

I looked to Ben. "If Ben decided he wanted to rebuild, I bet you'd be willing to do it at a discounted rate if you had the manpower, right?"

Larry nodded slowly. "Of course. Always give good rates to my friends."

"And you know Hurck can pull her own weight. I know she knows a few of the family that are just as good as she is with a hammer. What do you think about giving her a management position? Maybe give her a few of your guys and have her start her own crew? They could probably have a motel thrown up pretty quickly, don't you think?"

Larry took a thoughtful pull from his cigar. "More crews would mean more work. And you're right, she's basically already running my crew for me after a week. Running her own wouldn't be a huge step." He looked at Ben. "What do you say, Peck? Need that old roach trap thrown back up?"

Ben gave me a small smile before he turned to Larry. "Send a quote to my office and I'll have Mitchell approve it."

They both reached across the table and shook hands.

"So," Ed said after the handshake was done, "any

other news? I hear you're having some trouble with your sheep, Ben?"

"Who told you that?" Ben asked the butcher.

"Gary's brother. He stopped by the shop this morning for some sausage casings. Said something vague about something eating them."

Ben nodded. "Yeah. Weirdest thing. Kaga found one last night that looked like it had been bitten in half. He showed it to me this morning."

"Bitten in half?" I asked.

"That's what it looked like." Ben slid his cards together and placed them on the table before looking up to meet my eyes. "Ever see anything like that before?"

I thought about it for a moment. Any number of things could theoretically bite a sheep in half. "I could probably look into it for you," I said finally.

The others around the table looked at each other in confused silence.

Ben smiled at their confusion, and in a flat, conversational tone explained, "Hadn't you heard? Gary's our local fixer. No problem too big or monster too small."

They all turned to me and I grinned. "And I offer very competitive rates."

James is a South African born writer with an American accent, because children are cruel and laughed at the way he said "orange."

He was the last kid in his class to learn to read, so once that was remedied he quickly made up for lost time and read everything he could get his hands on. He now reads way better than all of them, except that one person who will always be smarter than him. They know who they are.

Eventually someone said, "Hey, James, read this fantasy novel." He did, and still hasn't managed to crawl out of that rabbit hole, though he has found others to fall into.

The first story he ever wrote was horrible but everyone pretended it was great, so now he can't feel good about himself unless someone is praising his work.

He lives in Utah with a dog and a growing collection of porch cats that he wishes would just go away.

www.jamesjakins.com

Thank you for reading *First Fixer*. If you enjoyed the story, please consider leaving a review or recommending the book to a friend.

If you'd like to learn more about the orcs of Summervale you can read the novel *Jack Bloodfist: Fixer*, starring Gary's son Jack as the new Fixer in town. Turn the page for a special preview.

And don't worry. Gary's gonna be back.

JACK BLOODFIST: FIXER
CHAPTER ONE

From the outside the building looks like any of the other skyscrapers in the city.

Maybe a little more modern, definitely more expensive. But still, the world headquarters of the Dongli Conglomerate mostly just looks like any other office building belonging to a billion-dollar company.

Because that's what it is. It houses the offices of some of the most powerful people on the planet.

What it also has, that very few other building in New York have, are cells.

Cells containing some of the most dangerous men and women in this world and others.

About halfway up the generous floor count, the cells start.

In one of these cells a man is kneeling. The spartan chamber holds him, a cot, a stainless steel toilet, and a camera that watches his every movement.

This is where, for the purposes of this story, we start.

His name is Arthur Shield. A long time ago, in a

whole other world, he was a high-ranking servant to a very powerful deity.

You might not believe it now, looking at him. A thick unkempt beard scrapes the worn concrete floor of his cell as he bows his body in prayer to his god.

He has done this almost everyday since being put in this cell.

He is a dangerous man, but without the blessings given him by his god, he is only as dangerous as any well-trained mortal can be.

That is why he prays. He has faith that if his prayers are long and loud enough, his lord Saban will hear him, and grant him the power he needs to escape his prison and seek revenge on those responsible for his crisis.

It turns out, that all you really need to get something you want is to pray for twenty years straight.

The camera that watches the small, round chamber catches everything.

The guards on duty watch the video feed, slightly confused at Shield's sudden change in behavior.

The man stands up, a grateful smile on his usually menacing face. They are more concerned, however, with the glowing eyes.

"Thank you," Arthur Shield says as he raises an open palm to the ceiling.

For an instant the same ethereal light that comes from his eyes glows around his upraised hand.

The camera dies and every alarm in the building begins to scream.

On every floor that houses prisoners, there is a room full of guards. Mostly they just play pool and watch whichever sporting event they can find on the TV that hangs above their mini fridge, but they are all trained killers.

Some of them used to reside in the very cells they now guard, but good behavior has its rewards.

Now, as alarms blare and radios scream out the floor and cell number, they all rush to arm themselves.

"It's Shield," a floor commander yells as he strap a vest and slings a rifle over his shoulder.

"He's a norm, right?" One of his men ask. There has been no precedent for them to expect anything from Shield.

"Thought so. Either way, shoot to kill."

There is a chorus of agreement right before they all march out of the combined break room/armory and into the hallway.

The lights of this floor have gone out. One florescent bulb flickers, trying to cling to life, before dropping the hall into darkness.

The guards click on lights attached to their vests and make their way to the cell of Arthur Shield.

There are no windows on the cells inside the Dongli Conglomerate building. There are prisoners in there that can kill with a look.

These prisoners are not even given cameras. It's just assumed they are alive. Or they're not. No one really seems to care enough to even consider Schrodinger or his cat.

The guard captain approaches the door, holding a hand up for silence. He places an ear to the thick steel door, in the vain hope that maybe he can hear something.

There is a snicker from one of his fellows and he casts a baleful eye toward the sound.

"Guns ready," he says.

There is the quiet clatter of rifles being shouldered.

He sidles over to the console next to the door, his rifle held with one hand, aiming with the rest of them.

There is the beep of a code being entered into a touch screen, then he scans a card that hangs on a lanyard from his neck.

The door slides open, the sound of well-oiled gears moving in the walls.

Their lights reveal nothing but the settling of dust from the destroyed ceiling. There is also a steady dripping sound.

A curious guard aims his light toward the sound. Hanging from the hole in the ceiling is a hand, the body attached to the hand still hidden in darkness.

Blood travels the length of the arm, dripping off one of the fingers.

The captain, at this sight, grabs at the radio on his shoulder.

This is when Arthur Shield attacks.

He drops from the hole in the ceiling, his body engulfed in a blue fire. The occupant of the cell above held firmly in burning fists.

None of the guards wait for orders. They open fire.

The bullets tear through the dead man Arthur is using as his defense, but none seem to hit him.

The corpse in his hands erupts in flame and he throws the burning figure into the nearest guard.

They all leap back, recovering quickly and raising guns again to fire on Shield.

He moves faster than any looking at him would

expect. His speed and strength seem too much for a man of his age.

The first guard he touches begins to scream in pain as the fire around Arthur's hands spreads. Soon the guard lies on the floor, the dancing blue of fire his only movement.

The other guards stand in shocked silence, though only for a moment. They are trained for these contingencies. For many of them, this is not the first time they have seen something like this.

Again, rifles are shouldered and the hallway erupts with the sound of gunfire.

The air around the prisoner shimmers with the same blue that fills his eyes and fuels the flames that cover him.

The bullets bounce of the shield of light that surrounds him, and the walls crack and shatter at the countless impacts.

Shield does not wait for the magazines to empty. He doesn't need to.

His eyes burn brighter as he jumps forward, the around him alive with the fire of his god's power and the sparks of ricocheting led.

His hand darts toward the nearest guard. He grabs the forearm and wrenches the rifle from the man's grasp.

He spins, leg flashing out, kicking the man in the chest.

The guard flies across the hallway, crumpling into a useless pile after connecting with a wall.

Shield faces the remaining guards and holds up his new weapon.

The guard captain has time to consider that maybe they shouldn't have trained this man to use a gun

A small area in the air in front of Arthur opens, allowing him to fire his rifle through his shield.

The rounds tear through the standing guards, painting the floor and walls with a handful of lives.

In the end, only the captain is alive. He sits on the floor, his back against the broken, blood-stained wall, gasping for breath.

"Stop," he wheezes, aiming his empty weapon with a shaky hand.

Arthur Shield turns to consider the man.

"No. If I stay, I'll be forced to kill more of you. It's really for the best that I leave." His voice is deep, commanding. It is the voice of a man that knows power.

"They'll stop you," the guard says.

"No, they won't." The prisoner steps back to the guard and places a blazing hand to his vest.

The guard manages a pained whine as the flames engulf his body.

Arthur does not stay to watch the man burn down to ash.

He walks calmly down the length of the corridor to where he knows elevators wait.

He flicks the security card he has stolen from a fallen guard over a security console.

The doors slide open with a soft "ding," and gentle, nondescript piano music filters into the silent hallway.

Arthur reaches inside the elevator, without stepping inside, and touches the card to a second security console.

After it acknowledges the card with another electronic tone he pushes the button for the top floor.

He steps back into the hallway and waits patiently as the doors close and the elevator rises.

The power to the elevator is cut before it gets more than three floors up, but that is more than enough for Shield.

He works his fingers between the closed doors and pries them open.

Before him is a fifty-foot drop through darkness. With another prayer on his lips he steps into air.

The lobby of the building is filled with guards now. Any guests have either been asked to leave, or locked in one of the many panic rooms the company has prepared for just such an occasion.

More security personnel are positioned outside the building to discourage anyone from wandering inside.

Several of the company's more specialized guards wait in the lobby as well, men and women trained to either use magics of some kind, or to disable the gifts of others.

They stand, dispersed around the lobby, some with artifacts of their various arts held at the ready. Others hold hands open, or closed, or in fighting stances.

They all hear the sound from above them: The crash of glass as the windows of the story above them burst and rain down into the plaza below.

Their prey sails through the air, landing squarely on the upturned face of a suit-wearing guard.

The Italian silk of the suit bursts into flames along with its owner.

The flash is bright enough that all watching cover their eyes.

Many of them recover quickly, but the brief moment

of distraction is all the escapee needs. Arthur Shield is gone.

For the rest of that day, and the following, they hunt him.

They do not find him. He hides in alleys and in stolen cars, walks through crowds that will never recognize him because his captors cannot afford to let the world know he exists.

He has no fear of them finding him. His god has returned to him. From a different world, with infinite chasms between them, Saban has found him and given him his power again.

Arthur Shield accepts this power and the mission that comes with it.

When he came to this world, he came seeking relics stolen from his temple. He will find them, and those that took them.

He will find the monsters, and he will kill them. Every. Last. One.

———

Now, the thing about goblin food is that it's greasy. I mean, shit-through-a-screen-door-at-thirty-paces greasy.

It pays to have family in the food service business. Free food, no matter how quickly it goes through me, is not something I would ever turn down.

And, for those in the know, goblin fry cooks are in very high demand. They mastered the American dining experience long before they ever set foot in the country.

It's an amazing heritage, let me tell you.

Luckily, if nothing else, it's a heritage that comes with a hole-in-the-wall diner.

Jack's Place is not named after me. The restaurant and I share a namesake. As do a couple dozen of my cousins, on both sides.

Our namesake, Jackson Smith, is a pretty popular guy. Comes with the territory, I suppose. He's a powerful wizard who also happens to be the savior of two large tribes. Every orc and goblin on the planet owes him their lives.

So, as a result, Jackson—and every variation of that name—will be the first choice every time a goblin or orc is born.

I know what you're thinking. What kind of wizard is named Jackson? Well, my understanding is that he was born in the Midwest United States somewhere, so Radagast probably wasn't a likely choice.

My real name is actually Garack. Good strong orc name. I did mention I was an orc right? No, I'm sure you caught that.

Garack was my father's name. He was the one responsible for uniting the tribes.

The one to blame for us having to move to Summervale, Virginia.

I was born in the old country, so when we came to the States my name was changed. Less likely to draw attention to the fact that we were not human, I guess.

Since the family settled, none of my cousins have even bothered with traditional names. All Jacks and Jills.

It's actually pretty amazing how quickly people can adapt to a new culture.

Sorry, probably too much info up front for you. Let me start over.

My name is Jack Bloodfist, and I'm an orc. Well, half-orc. Mom was a goblin. Love is blind, right?

I inherited more of the orcish looks, though, so I just say I'm an orc.

And despite what you might be picturing, I'm not some hideous, malformed mutant.

I'd be lying if I said there were websites dedicated to my beauty, but I'm definitely not the ugliest in the family. Not by human standards, at least. And those are the only ones that really count in this world.

Thanks to the small, slender frame of the goblin I'm not as much of a hulking brute as some of my full-blooded orc cousins. In fact, my size is pretty close to within the normal range for most humans.

There are other things I have to deal with that might give me away. The tusks, for one.

Like most of the other orcs in the area, I trim those. They grow back pretty fast, but a good grinding every two days or so keeps them from sticking up over the top lip.

I also grow a decent beard, which I let grow as much as possible to hopefully hide my fairly noticeable underbite.

My ears also point a little bit, but less than some of the elves I've met over the years. And not really enough that anyone's ever actually commented.

Hair? Well, unfortunately I inherited my mother's hair. Goblin hair is almost as greasy as their food, so I keep that dome bald.

Mostly I do everything I can to move around unnoticed.

I had to for my job back then.

As you might imagine, when you suddenly transplant a large horde of goblins and a decent-sized orc fist into suburban Virginia, problems arise.

Someone needs to play the part of middle-man. Fix any issues that may pop up. Smooth over that good old-fashioned tribal violence with the local PD. All that fun stuff.

That's what I did. My father did it until his death five years ago, then I took over.

At the time I felt pretty proud of it. Even had cards made. I thought I was an essential part of the community.

I even took my responsibilities pretty seriously. I had an old ratty suit I threw on anytime I had official business to take care of.

This usually led to an interrogation from my mother and her father, who ran Jack's Place.

The fact that I also wore the suit on any dates I happened to have, as rare as they were, meant they got excited.

Most goblins don't live to see their grandkids be born, so Ma wanted that, and Gramps wanted to be the first goblin to meet his great-grandkids.

Honestly, I felt no regret in disappointing them.

"Meeting lady friend tonight?" Gramps asked me in his broken English from behind the counter. He stood on a custom ledge that ran the length of it so he almost stood eye level with me as I sat there.

I focused on the massive plate of greasy potatoes, meat, and eggs, mostly gone.

I had only one errand for the day. Just one of those little things the family liked me to take care of so they didn't have to.

"Maybe later," I answered truthfully. I never knew when the lady friend in question might be up for something, though I never had actually told Gramps there was only one. He assumed I was the town lady-killer. Which was ridiculous.

"Work then?" he asked.

It wasn't hard to hear the curiosity in his voice. My work always had the possibility of being a gold mine for gossip. Goblins love gossip.

"You remember Devin?" I asked.

He gave me a blank stare in response.

"Snaga?" I said, taking a minute to recall his name before the move.

"Ah, Shakill's oldest?"

"Karen, yeah." My father's sister had also changed her name. Gramps was really the only one in the families that had any problem remembering that we had to fit in.

None of us really tried to correct him. It's not that orcs or goblins have a traditional respect-your-elders philosophy. It's all about strength. As a result, most didn't live very long.

Gramps was almost eighty. That was practically unheard of for anyone that had grown up in the homeland. My generation might expect that to be almost normal, but not those that came before us. We didn't have to deal with any of the shit this old man had lived through.

So everyone in the community respected the old bastard. They also like his cooking. That helps.

"Yes, yes, Karen." He waved an annoyed hand at my correction. "What about the boy?"

I shoveled a pile of greasy potatoes into my mouth and spoke around the food. "Moving back into town, bringing his fiancée with."

Devin had been a few years older than me, so I had never known him very well.

Being a little more orc than me, he'd also taken up with the local street toughs, though Summervale didn't really have anything worthy of his time, so when he was older he moved to New York.

If I'm being honest, I think he just moved out there to become an actor. I mean, seriously, why else does anyone move to New York? Stand-up?

"So you, what? Set up house for them?" Gramps asked.

I nodded as I pulled some egg out of my beard. "Got a trailer ready for them, just need to hand them the keys."

This was something I did a lot. Whenever someone decided to move back home they had a place to stay until they got their feet underneath them.

My landlady always kept two or three of her units vacant for me. She's a nice lady, for a gnome.

"This fiancée," Gramps asked, "she pretty?"

"No idea. Never met her."

"If she pretty, you should steal her. He doesn't need a wife. You do."

"I'll take that into consideration."

"Good. How's the food today?" he asked.

"Good as always, sir." I shoveled more grease into my mouth.

"Damn right it's good. Fresh-laid eggs, boy. Much better than store-bought shit."

I nodded my somber agreement as I finished the last of the plate.

"So, I make lunch for the orc and your future wife?"

"Sounds good. I'll send them by."

"When they arrive?"

"I'm meeting them at my place in…" I pulled my phone out of my pocket and checked the time. "Shit, ten minutes. I'd better go."

I wiped egg yolk and grease out of my beard and tossed the napkin on my plate.

"Tell Ma I said hi," I shouted over my shoulder.

The old goblin waved a dismissive hand as he started to clean up my breakfast.

Once outside, the humid summer air hit me and I regretted my commitment to the suit.

Jack's Place is on the outskirts of Summervale, right off the freeway.

On one side is the main road that runs into town, lined with gas stations and run-down apartment buildings. Another is the rarely busy aforementioned freeway, and every other side is flanked by thick groves of Virginia pine. At least I think that's what they are. Could be maple. You know what, let's just say trees.

I crossed the parking lot, the sun-baked asphalt hot under the thin soles of my worn shoes, and unlocked my old Cadillac.

It wasn't the greatest car in the world, probably very far from it, but I loved it.

My phone vibrated as I climbed behind the wheel.

"Jack," I said as I answered without looking at the

caller info.

"Bloodfist," a terse voice said, "got a body at the morgue. Need you to ID the bastard."

"Well, good morning to you too, Denny," I said to the woman on the other end.

"What did I say about that?" Her voice carried its normal aggression.

"Sorry. Good morning, Detective Halldorson." I tried my best to oversell the formality,

"When can you come in?" she asked, tone just as angry despite my etiquette. "Fresh orc corpse in the morgue."

"Ah, shit. Who is it? One of the Jacks?" I was more annoyed than anything.

I'm basically related to every orc on the planet. Not directly. There are three different clans in our fist, but they're all basically family.

All that really means is that anytime one of us bites it, it's a death in the family. Which would suck if we were more sentimental.

Still, it's kind of sad if you think about it too much. In just a few generations there won't be any real orcs left. That alone makes each death hurt a little more. Well, it should, anyway.

It also makes our natural tendencies to look for trouble seem a whole lot dumber than they might have in the homeland.

"If I knew who he was I wouldn't ask you to ID him. I'd ask you to find their next of kin. You do remember how this works, right?"

"So, no ID then?"

She let out a long sigh, "No. No ID. Farmer found

the body in his field this morning. When can you come in?"

I checked the time on my car's clock. "I have an appointment in a few minutes. Shouldn't take more than half an hour. That okay?"

"Yeah, that's fine. I'll keep him cold for you." She hung up before I could say anything else.

Denelle Halldorson is not the friendliest individual. I do still consider her a friend, even if she doesn't always share the opinion.

She's always been really good about keeping us informed about any situations that should probably be kept away from the general population. She's even willing to help if you need to cover something up. Really good at it too.

She's had plenty of practice. Living in the same city for two hundred years without anyone noticing takes some skill. I was just happy she was willing to use those skills to help me do my job.

I returned my phone to my pocket as I pulled into the trailer park.

I know. You were expecting me to have some smoky office downtown. I wish. I can barely afford the rent for my trailer. The families would never spring for an office.

An old sedan was parked in front of my trailer. I pulled into my tiny driveway and studied the woman standing on my front porch.

Tall, slender, and blond. Just missing the red dress.

I couldn't see her face, because her hands were cupped over it as she tried to see through the dirty window on my door.

www.ingramcontent.com/pod-product-compliance
Lightning Source LLC
Chambersburg PA
CBHW030559130626
46552CB00006B/2599